THIS IS A STORY

words by
John Schu

illustrations by
Lauren Castillo

CANDLEWICK PRESS

This is a story for Amy Krouse Rosenthal, Molly O'Neill,
Kate DiCamillo, Lauren Castillo, and you.
JS

For John Schu and all librarians.
You make the world a better place!
LC

This is a word.

Sea

In the warm ocean, among the waving sea-grass meadow, an eye like a small black bead is watching... fish dart by. Where does it belong to?

SEA HORSE— one of the shyest fish in the sea,

This is a word on a page.

In the warm ocean,
among the waving sea-grass meadows,
an eye like a small black bead
is watching the fish dart by.
Who does it belong to?

SEA HORSE —
one of the shyest fish in the sea.

This is a page in a book.

This is a book on a shelf . . .

waiting.

Look at the world.
The world is full of humans.

Sometimes humans need help . . .

connecting.

This is a book.

This is a reader.

Here are some more readers

with minds full of questions . . .

with ideas to explore . . .

with hopes for the future . . .

with imaginations ready to spark.

They all have hearts

that can grow . . .

endlessly.

This is our world of reading.

It starts small,

but it shows us where to begin.

This is a story.

And it helps us understand . . .

everything!